S0-AJX-167

Puss in Boots

and other bedtime stories

Contents

ARCTURUS

Puss in Boots

Once there was a miller who had three sons.
When he died, he left the mill to his eldest son
and his donkey to his second son. The third son
was not so lucky, he was only left the family cat.

"I'm sorry, Puss," said the miller's son. "I don't
know what we are going to do. How can I even
look after you with no job and no money?"

"Don't worry," said the cat. "Just give me some
boots and a bag and we'll be fine."

Puss pulled on the boots, filled the bag with
lettuce leaves and marched off to a meadow.

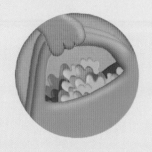

Before long a little rabbit hopped over to the bag and began to nibble at the lettuce. In a flash, Puss scooped up the bag and hurried off to the King's palace.

When he saw the King, Puss swept off his hat and bowed low.

"Your majesty," he said, "may I present you with this very fine rabbit, a gift from my master, the Marquis of Carrabas?"

The King frowned. "I don't believe I know him," he said, "but you deserve a treat from the palace kitchens."

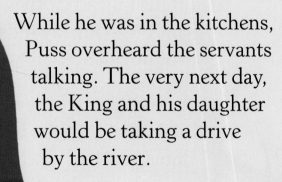

While he was in the kitchens, Puss overheard the servants talking. The very next day, the King and his daughter would be taking a drive by the river.

Puss returned to his master. In the morning, he told him, "Go for a swim in the river. If anyone asks, say that your name is the Marquis of Carrabas."

The miller's son did as Puss said. He went to the river, took off his ragged clothes, and jumped in. Puss quickly hid the clothes in the bushes.

A minute later, the royal carriage drove past with the King and his daughter the Princess inside. "Stop the carriage!" cried the King. "Why, it is the clever cat who came to see me yesterday."

Puss heaved a great sigh. "I wish, your Majesty, I could present my master, but while he was swimming in the river, a thief stole all his clothes!"

At once, the King asked for a suit of fine clothes to be brought from the palace. The miller's son got dressed behind the bushes and shyly came forward.

"My dear Marquis," beamed the King, "may I present my daughter, the Princess? Do come and ride with us."

Puss scampered on ahead. He saw a man making hay in a meadow. "The King will be here in a moment," Puss told him. "My master, the Marquis of Carrabas, will be very grateful if you tell the King that he owns all the land around here."

"I can do that," said the man, "but let's hope the ogre who lives in that castle doesn't hear me. The land is his."

Puss then hurried to the ogre's castle. When the huge ogre opened the door, Puss spoke up boldly. "I have heard," he said, "that you are a great magician. Is that true?"

"Come in," replied the ogre, "and I will show you!"

In a flash, he turned himself into a fierce lion.

"Well," said Puss, "I'm sure it's easy for a big, strong ogre to become a big, strong lion. But could you become a tiny, weak mouse?"

"Just watch me!" roared the ogre.

Puss pounced! He munched up the mouse and looked around. "This castle is the perfect home for my master, the Marquis of Carrabas," he said.

When the King saw the castle, he was very impressed. "The Marquis is just the kind of young man I should like my daughter to marry," he said. The Princess agreed!

So Puss, the Princess, and the miller's son lived happily ever after.

The Lion and the Mouse

One day a little mouse was scampering through the jungle when he bumped into something big and yellow.

"Eeek!" squeaked the little mouse.

"Rrrrrroar!" replied the big, yellow thing. It was a lion!

The little mouse turned to run away as fast as his tiny feet could carry him, but the lion stretched out his paw and put it down firmly on the mouse's tail.

"Not so fast, Little Mouse," growled the lion. "You'll make a tasty afternoon snack."

"Oh please, please, Sir," squeaked the mouse, "don't eat me. I promise, if you let me go, I will be your friend and help you whenever you need me."

The lion roared with laughter. "When would I ever need you?" he chortled. "But you've cheered me up today, so go on your way, Little Mouse."

"Thank you, my friend," replied the mouse.

The very next day, as the lion was snoozing after lunch, some hunters crept up and captured him in a net. Although he roared and fought with all his strength, the mighty beast could not get free.

"We'll leave him here tonight," said the hunters, "and take him away in the morning."

The hunters left. Night fell, and the exhausted lion lay still. Suddenly, he heard a tiny sound. "I knew you would need me one day, my friend," whispered the little mouse.

"I am much bigger and stronger than you," sighed the lion, "and I couldn't get free. What could you possibly do?"

"Only this," smiled the mouse, and he began to gnaw at the ropes holding the net to the ground. Very quickly, his sharp little teeth cut them in two. In minutes, the lion was free.

It just goes to show that even the strongest person needs a friend sometimes, and someone very small can make a BIG difference.

Chicken Little

There once was a little chick called Chicken Little. One day as he was scratching about under an old oak tree, an acorn fell on his head. Chicken Little didn't see the acorn.

"Ouch!" he cried.

"The sky is falling down! I must go and tell the King."

Chicken Little ran through the farmyard, where he met Henny Penny.

"Oh, Henny Penny," cried Chicken Little, "the sky is falling down and I'm going to tell the King."

"Cluck! Cluck! I will come too," said Henny Penny.

Chicken Little and Henny Penny were just going through the farmyard gate when they met Cocky Locky.

"Oh, Cocky Locky," cried Chicken Little, "the sky is falling down and we're going to tell the King."

"Doodle-doo! I will come too," said Cocky Locky.

Chicken Little, Henny Penny, and Cocky Locky were hurrying past the pond when they met Ducky Lucky and Goosey Loosey.

"Oh, Ducky Lucky, Goosey Loosey," cried Chicken Little, "the sky is falling down and we're going to tell the King."

"Quack! Quack! Honk! Honk! We will come too," said Ducky Lucky and Goosey Loosey.

Chicken Little, Henny Penny, Cocky Locky, Ducky Lucky, and Goosey Loosely were turning the corner when they met Turkey Lurkey.

"Oh, Turkey Lurkey," cried Chicken Little, "the sky is falling down and we're going to tell the King."

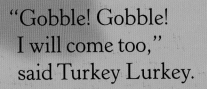

"Gobble! Gobble! I will come too," said Turkey Lurkey.

Chicken Little, Henny Penny, Cocky Locky, Ducky Lucky, Goosey Loosey, and Turkey Lurkey had come to the edge of the wood when they met Foxy Loxy.

"Oh, Foxy Loxy," cried Chicken Little, "the sky is falling down and we're going to tell the King."

"Then come with me," said Foxy Loxy.
"I will take you to the King."

The birds all followed him and he took them
into the wood where his family was waiting
for dinner.

Poor Chicken Little, Henny Penny,
Cocky Locky, Ducky Lucky, Goosey Loosey,
and Turkey Lurkey were never seen again.

And the fox family lived happily ever after,
although ever so many acorns
fell on their heads.

Tom Thumb

Long ago there lived a woodsman and his wife who had no children. "If only we had a child to help me in the forest and be company for you in the house," said the woodsman sadly.

"If we had a child of our own," replied his wife, "I wouldn't mind if he or she was only as big as your thumb."

A few years later, their dreams came true, and they had a tiny baby. He really was tiny. His mother and father fed him the best food they could buy, but he never grew any bigger than his father's thumb. They named him Thomas, but his nickname soon became Tom Thumb.

Young Tom Thumb was a lively boy. He was full of plans and schemes, and his tiny body never seemed to stop him.

One day, he overheard his parents talking. "I'm not as young as I was," his father said. "It's getting harder to work in the forest on my own. It's a pity that young Tom can't help me."

Tom thought about this. He was upset that his parents didn't think he would be able to look after them as they got older.

The next day, when his father had set off into the forest, Tom jumped up on to the table where his mother was making bread and said, "I'm going to help Dad today. Please harness up the horse so that I can drive the cart and take logs into town for him."

"Don't be silly, dear," said his mother, "and mind you don't fall in that flour! The horse is big and strong. You would never manage to control her."

"Please, Mother," Tom pleaded.

His mother was doubtful, but she knew
that Tom was a clever lad, so she did
as he asked. When the horse was
harnessed, however, she frowned.
"It's too dangerous," she said.
"I can't let you do this."

Tom smiled. "I'm not going to use the reins,"
he explained. "Put me in the horse's ear.
I'll tell her what to do instead."

Tom's mother placed him carefully in the horse's
warm ear. "Come on, old Beauty," he whispered.
"We're going into the forest. You know the way.
I'll tell you when to stop."

To Tom's mother's
amazement, the
horse trotted off.

As Tom went along, he passed two men on the road. They owned a traveling show. "Did you see that?" one man said to the other. "A horse and cart with no driver!"

"Let's follow it," said his friend. "We could use a clever horse in our show."

The men crept closer. It was then that they saw the tiny boy whispering in the horse's ear. That was even better! People would pay a fortune to see a tiny boy like Tom Thumb!

Tom's father was amazed to see the horse and cart, but before he could speak, the two men hurried forward.

"What a fine boy you have," they said. "We will give you fifty gold pieces if you will let him come with us."

"Never!" cried the woodsman, but Tom whispered in his ear. "They are tricksters. Let's trick them! Take the money and I will escape from them later and come home."

That's exactly what
happened. Tom's father took
the money, and the two men took Tom,
but that evening, Tom escaped into some long
grass and the men could not find him anywhere.
Then Tom hid in a cart that was going back
towards his home and strolled in to dinner
right on time!

How happy Tom's
parents were to see their
boy! Ever afterwards, *little*
Tom was always known as
a very *big* help to his family.

The Perfect Pirate

Once upon a time, a pirate family lived in a tumbledown cottage near the sea. They were Pa Pirate, Ma Pirate and little Petey Pirate.

 Ma and Pa Pirate were feared from one shore of the Swirly Sea to the other. They hoped that little Petey would grow up to be a perfect pirate, too. When he was only a baby, they began to teach him pirate ways.

"Say 'Aaaaaaaarrrgh!' Petey," begged Ma Pirate.

"Doo doo, da da!" cooed little Petey.

 Ma and Pa looked at each other. "He's very young," said Ma Pirate. "We must give him time."

But as little Petey grew, he didn't become more fearsome. He was a well-mannered child, always smiling. Ma and Pa were upset that their beloved son seemed far too polite to be a proper pirate.

"Petey, how many times do I have to tell you?" his father would say. "You don't put your goblet away on the shelf like that. Hurl it on the floor like this!"

"But that makes a mess," said Petey.

As he grew up, Petey loved reading, nature, drawing, music and dancing. He showed no interest at all in fighting, swearing, or going to bed with his seaboots on.

Ma and Pa Pirate had a serious talk.

"There's only one thing to do," said Pa Pirate. "We must take him on a voyage. The boy has pirate blood. When he's on the deck of a ship, with a fierce sou'westerly blowing in his ears, he'll know he is a pirate."

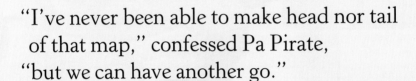

"I agree," said Ma. "We'll take Old Bartholomew's treasure map with us and look for his buried booty."

"I've never been able to make head nor tail of that map," confessed Pa Pirate, "but we can have another go."

The Pirate parents loved being at sea again.
They stomped around the deck, crying,
"Avast me hearties!" and "Sluice me scuppers!"
Petey curled up on the deck, looking pale.

After a few days, Petey stopped feeling seasick
and took an interest – in studying shipworms
and drawing clouds.

Ma and Pa sailed and sailed but they couldn't
find the treasure. Neither of them knew how
to read the map!

"You've got the map the wrong way up," Petey told his mother. "And you're going in the wrong direction," he said to his father.

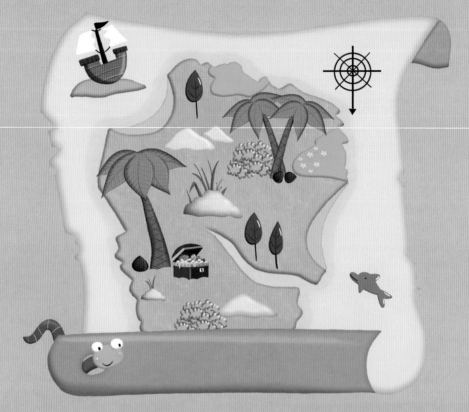

Ma and Pa looked at each other. They knew their chance of finding the treasure was very small. Following Petey's advice couldn't make things worse.

Two days later, the Pirate family was sitting on the beach of a tiny island. The Pirate parents gazed open-mouthed at the cascade of sparkling jewels tumbling from Old Bartholomew's sea chest.

"I don't believe it!"
gasped Pa Pirate.
"We're rich!"

Ma Pirate gave Petey a hug. "Our Petey
may not be fearsome, or quick with a cutlass,"
she said, "but he's the best treasure-finder
in all of the Swirly Sea,
and *that* means he is
a *perfect* pirate."

ARCTURUS

This edition published in 2013 by Arcturus Publishing Limited
26/27 Bickels Yard, 151–153 Bermondsey Street,
London SE1 3HA

Copyright © 2013 Arcturus Publishing Limited
All rights reserved.

ISBN: 978-1-84858-865-3
CH002601US
Supplier 15, Date 1212, Print run 2275

Printed in China